This material originally published
as two separate titles:

Teddy Bears 123
Teddy Bears ABC
Includes additional pages.

This edition published in 2001 by Brimax
an imprint of Octopus Publishing Group Ltd
2-4 Heron Quays, London E14 4JP
© Octopus Publishing Group Ltd
Printed and bound in China

learn with me

Teddy Bears ABC 123

BRIMAX

Aa

A is for acrobat
Tumbling across the floor;
The teddies clap together
And loudly cheer for more.

Bb

B is for bicycle,
The teddies like to ride;
They race each other down the path
Then cycle side by side.

Cc

C is for cat
High up on the wall;
Sam wants to stop and say, "Hello!"
But he is far too small.

Dd

D is for dolphin
Swimming in the sea;
The teddies watch him play all day,
As happy as can be.

Ee

E is for elephant
Living at the zoo;
The teddies like to watch him
As he eats the whole day through!

Ff

F is for fair,
The teddies have such fun;
They ride upon the merry-go-round
And wave to everyone.

Gg

G is for gloves
Ben wears in the snow;
He likes to watch his friends
As they're skating to and fro.

Hh

H is for holly
Above the Christmas tree;
Sam is wrapping presents
For his friends, on Christmas Eve.

Ii

I is for igloo
Made on a snowy day;
The teddies put on hats and scarves
Then run outside to play.

Jj

J is for juggler
Throwing balls so high;
The teddy bears all sit and watch
As they seem to touch the sky.

Kk

K is for kangaroo
Bouncing all around;
The teddies like to watch him
Jump high up off the ground.

Ll

L is for lake
Where the teddies like to be;
They watch the boats go sailing by
As happy as can be.

Mm

M is for mouse
That runs across the floor;
Rosie tries to catch him
As he slips out through the door.

Nn

N is for nest
With baby birds inside,
The teddies like to watch them
As they are learning how to fly.

Oo

O is for owl
Sleeping in a tree;
The teddies must not wake him up
So they sit quietly.

Pp

P is for picnic
With lots of things to eat;
And all the teddy bears agree
It is a special treat.

Qq

Q is for queen,
Rosie pretends to be;
She sits upon her golden throne
For all her friends to see.

Rr

R is for river,
Flowing to the sea;
Fishing can be lots of fun
The teddy bears agree.

Ss

S is for sandcastle,
Ben builds by the sea;
Sam and Rosie want to help
And soon there are three.

Tt

T is for trumpet
All the teddies hear,
The trumpet playing loudly
As the band marches near.

Uu

U is for umbrella
To keep us dry from rain;
The teddy bears take cover
Until the sun comes out again.

Vv

V is for violin,
Polly plays a tune;
The others tap their feet,
They'll all be dancing soon.

Ww

W is for wigwam,
The teddies build for fun;
They like to look like Indians
Playing in the sun.

Xx

X is for xylophone
Rosie likes to play;
Her friends all sing together
As Rosie taps away.

Yy

Y is for yacht,
The teddies sail away;
They like to float around the lake
On a sunny day.

Zz

Z is for zebra,
He gallops round and round;
Sam and Polly watch him
As he runs along the ground.

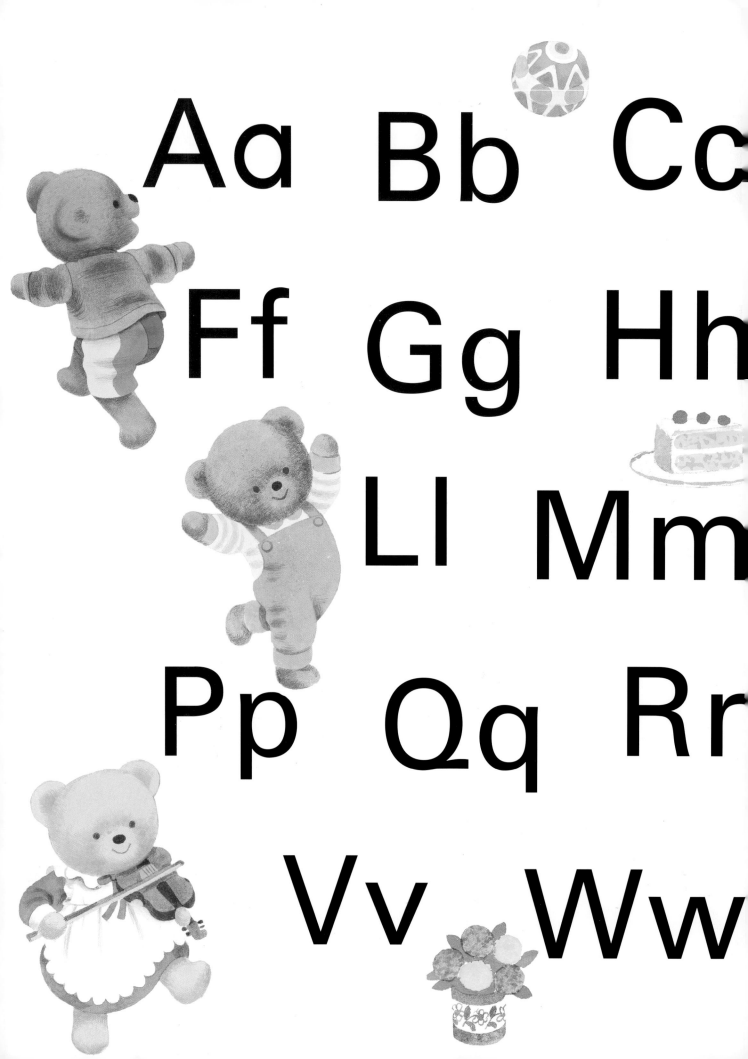

Aa Bb Cc

Ff Gg Hh

Ll Mm

Pp Qq Rr

Vv Ww

Dd Ee

Ii Jj Kk

Nn Oo

Ss Tt Uu

Xx Yy Zz

One teddy bear is cycling.
The wheels turn round and round;
Up the hill, then down again,
He races all around.

Two teddy bears are in the park,
There's lots to see and do,
They swing and slide all morning
Then play ball all afternoon.

Three teddy bears are by the sea,
The sun is warm and bright;
When they have had their picnic lunch
They like to fly their kite.

Four teddy bears are gardening,
They help to clear the weeds;
There is a lot of work to do
Before they plant their seeds.

4

Five teddy bears are skipping,
The rope turns round and round;
They count each jump they make,
As they skip along the ground.

5

Six teddies like to rollerskate
Together in the sun;
Up and down the path they go
Having lots of fun.

6

Seven teddy bears are climbing
High up in a tree;
They reach the top, then look around,
There is so much to see.

7

Eight teddy bears are cleaning,
There is a lot to do;
They dust and clean and polish,
Working the whole day through.

8

Nine teddy bears play in the snow;
They like to skate and slide
Together down a snowy slope;
They all enjoy their ride.

9

Ten teddy bears are warm in bed
The moon is shining bright.
They like to hear a story
In the middle of the night.

3

6

7

9

10